TOUGH AS
OLD BOOTS

RACHEL ANDERSON

Illustrated by
LINDA BIRCH

HEINEMANN · LONDON

William Heinemann Ltd
Michelin House, 81 Fulham Road
London SW3 6RB

LONDON   MELBOURNE   AUCKLAND

First published in 1991
Text © Rachel Anderson
Illustrations © 1991 Linda Birch
The right of Rachel Anderson to be identified as author of this work
has been asserted by her in accordance with the Copyright, Designs
and Patents Act 1988.
ISBN 0 434 97663 6
Produced by Mandarin Offset
Printed in Hong Kong

A school pack of SUPERCHAMPS 13–18
is available from
Heinemann Educational Books
ISBN 0 435 00092 6

1 Getting Ready

I HAD THIS Grandma, see. Not that I knew I'd got her till she came to live with us.

One morning my Mum said to me,

'Eat up your flakes Joe, or you'll be late again. And don't forget your sandwiches, on the table there. Your Grandma's coming tomorrow.'

I said, 'Yes, Mum.'

'So if I'm not here when you get back, you'll have to let yourself in. You know where the key is, don't you?'

I said, 'OK, Mum.'

She said, 'Joe, you're not listening. Stop reading that cereal packet and get a move on.'

I said, 'Who took my trainers? Somebody's moved them! I know I took them off somewhere just near here.'

'If you put your things away properly, Joe, you wouldn't keep losing them. Anyway, you can't wear trainers on a day like this.'

It was only raining a very little bit. I found my trainers under the armchair in the front room. Somebody must have hidden them there on purpose to annoy me.

'Bye, Mum!' I said and ran off to meet my mate Slane down on the corner by the supermarket. Then I remembered my sandwiches. I had to dash back to pick them up off the kitchen table while Slane kept the bus driver talking to stop the bus going without me. So what with one thing and another there wasn't time to think any more about a grandmother till I got home after school.

Dad and Mum were both back early from work. I didn't have to go looking for the key under the mat after all.

My Dad was upstairs shifting furniture. My Mum was upstairs painting walls. They both looked very busy.

'Hey, that's my bed!' I said when I realised.

Dad was trying to shift it across the top landing. He'd got jammed halfway. He couldn't move up or down, backwards or forwards. He was looking out through the bed-springs wondering what to do next. I thought he looked a bit like a rabbit in a cage.

'Give your Dad a hand, Joe, will you?'
my Mum called to me. 'He'll never
manage on his own.' She had pink paint
all up her arms.

In the end we managed to get my bed
shifted. Then my football posters had to
come down. All my stuff went in the
little room next to the bathroom, that's
more like a cupboard.

I said, 'Why are we moving all my stuff?'

'To make it tidy for your grandmother, of course,' said my Mum. 'We've got to be ready before she comes.'

I said, 'I don't know anything about a grandmother.'

'Of course you do,' said my Mum. 'I told you this morning. I *knew* you weren't listening.'

'I heard you. I thought you meant Nana Pat.'

Of course I knew all about Mum's mum, though Nana Pat's not what you'd think of as a real grandmother. She looks quite young and behaves young. Well, that's what my Mum says.

Nana Pat lives in a hacienda-style retirement sunshine home in Spain. She dances flamenco, goes to parties every night, and wears lots of make-up. You could almost take them for sisters, my Mum and my Nana Pat: well, that's what my Mum says anyway. But my friend Slane says they both look middle-aged, just like her Aunty Vee.

'It's the strain,' said my Mum. 'Of tidying up after Joe; that made me old before my time.' But she gave me a hug so I don't think she meant it.

Mum handed me a pile of pink curtains covered in pink flowers and a box of plastic curtain hooks. There were curtains in my room already. But it seems that this other grandmother wasn't going to like the kind of curtains which were a bit torn where Slane and I tried to make a hammock out of them, or a bit spotty where we'd used them to mop up some paint.

'Why not?' I said. 'They're nice curtains. Got that lived-in look.'

'Maybe. But not for an old lady. We've got to do our very best for her.'

I wondered why, if we'd never done it before.

'Because she's been poorly. She needs looking after. And there's no-one else now that your aunt can't have her any more.'

It was Dad's mum this time. I said, 'I mean, I never knew about another grandmother.' One grandmother, who did flamenco dancing, had always seemed just about right.

'Well you know now,' said my Mum. 'So I hope you'll behave nicely when she arrives, and remember to be as tidy as you can.'

'And I'm afraid the cat'll have to sleep out,' said my Dad. 'She's always been

poorly with her breathing and the fur won't help.'

Poor old cat. Poor old me, too.

I wasn't at all sure about this person coming to live with us. As I explained to my friend Slane, that poky little cupboard next to the bathroom was very small. There wasn't even enough space to stick up my best football posters. I had to leave most of them rolled up under the bed.

'Hardly even as big as a hen-coop, is it?' I said. 'How can she expect me to keep tidy in here?'

Slane agreed. 'So when's she coming?'

'Soon,' I said.

'You better tell them,' said Slane, 'that you're going to complain.'

'I *have* complained!' I said. 'Dad said I mustn't be selfish. And she's only a poor old lady on her last legs.'

'Not to your parents. I mean
complain to the proper authorities. Tell
them it's cruel to a young boy, to put
him into this little room where you
won't be able to grow properly, not if
you can't stretch out your arms and
legs. I mean, if they're not allowed to do
it to pigs and hens, they shouldn't be
allowed to do it to *you*.'

I thanked Slane for her support and
said I'd definitely think about it, though
I wasn't sure who the proper authorities
were.

2 Welcome!

MY MUM'S GOT this thing about being tidy. She really hates mess. It makes her go pale. She goes on at me about tidiness because she still thinks I don't understand what it means. Of course I do. It's just that I *like* my room that way.

When I got back from school it wasn't just my own poky room that was untidy. Our whole house was untidy. Even I could see that. So could Slane.

I knew it couldn't be *my* mess because I'd only just stepped in through the back door so I hadn't had time to make any, had I?

For a wonderful moment, I thought
Mum must have had a character change.

There were clothes draped over the
bannisters like at a jumble sale,

newspapers scattered across the hall floor, a half-drunk cup of tea on the hall table, and biscuit crumbs everywhere.

It looked almost like the corporation tip up the far end of town. The only thing missing, so Slane said, was the seagulls flying around in circles overhead.

'Mum!' I called. 'I'm home! What's all this mess about? What're you *doing*?'

But it wasn't Mum who'd made it. Mum was in her neat and tidy kitchen quietly making a pot of tea. She was a bit pale.

'Hello, Joe dear,' she said giving me a vague welcome-home hug more as though I was a bit of furniture that needed dusting than her son. 'Your Grandma's arrived. Isn't that nice?'

I said, 'Mum, there's stuff all over the

hall.'

'Yes dear, I know. Your Grandma's been unpacking one or two things.'

She threw a despairing look at the clothes and crumbs scattered along the hall. 'And she's only been here twenty minutes! I hope we'll manage.'

'Looks nice,' I said. In fact it was better than nice. In twenty minutes, this grandmother had managed to do what often takes me a whole week. She'd made the place look homely.

'Lived in. Friendly,' I said.

There was a funny noise from upstairs, like heavy thumping.

'She's upstairs resting, is she?' I said. I knew old people needed lots of rest because you often see them sitting about on park benches looking half asleep.

'Resting!' Mum said. 'You must be joking! She's got more energy than you and Slane put together! I just hope she doesn't *hurt* herself.'

I wondered how anybody could hurt themselves settling into a new room.

So Slane went home and I went upstairs to have a look.

She was lots older than I expected, and smaller too, even smaller than me. She looked so frail that she might easily fall over in a puff of wind.

I said, 'Hello, Grandma.'

She didn't answer. It wasn't so much because she was deaf – though I realised she might be deaf as well – but because of the hammering.

3 Settling in

TAPPY, TAP. WHAM. Bash. Tappy, hit. Splutter, splat. She was trying to fix some big nails into the wall and she wasn't very good at it. Each time she missed, another shower of plaster fell down and the lamp on the ceiling jumped.

Mum doesn't really like me even using sticky tape on the walls because she says it leaves grey marks on the paintwork, let alone drawing pins. She says they make little holes. But not nearly such big holes as nails make.

'Looks good,' I said. With all the plaster dust, and the new cracks, and Dad's carpentry tools spread about, it looked more like a workshop than a bedroom.

I wished *I'd* thought to make it into a workshop when it was my bedroom.

Dad's hammer was heavy for Grandma's knobbly little hands, and she was wheezing from the effort.

'I'll do it for you,' I said.

Grandma said, 'I would have asked *her* to do it. But I didn't want to disturb her. She's got more than enough tidying up after your father. He always *was* a difficult boy.'

I hammered in three nails and Grandma hung three football posters from them.

'To cover up the pink,' said Grandma. 'What a silly colour to paint a bedroom.

Nobody could live with that, could they? Looks like a hospital. So I thought we'd pop these nice pictures over the pink.'

'They're football posters, Grandma.' My football posters. She must have found them under my bed.

'And all such nice-looking young men, aren't they?'

She didn't like the flowery curtains either. She was right. Flowers should be in gardens. We took them down.

My relatives, specially Nana Pat, usually say, 'How you've grown, Joe!' as though they're surprised.

This one didn't. While I was up on the chair seeing to the curtains, she said, 'Well, you're not much of a size, Joseph, are you? Never mind, duckie. Stay small and you can always try for a job as a jockey.'

Nobody calls me Joseph, not even my
teacher. It's always Joe. I liked the
sound of Joseph. It was more grownup
than Joe.

I liked my new Grandma.

4 It's tea-time

Downstairs, Mum had cleared up and was laying the tea-table.

'I was right about the paint,' I said. 'She doesn't like it.'

Grandma came wheezing breathlessly into the kitchen and tottered as fast as her bendy legs would take her across to the table.

'Oh, but my dear girl!' she cried. I'd never heard my Mum called a dear girl before. It sounded funny. She might be a dear, but she wasn't much of a girl.

'Dear girl! You must let me help you all I can!' said Grandma and grabbed the pile of plates with the tomato ketchup bottle balanced on top from my Mum.

It wasn't her fault that she didn't get as far as the table before her legs got in a muddle underneath her. And it wasn't her fault that the cat came in and got in the way. The plates crashed down around it and the ketchup bottle splatted on the floor. Poor cat. It ran for its life through the back door.

Mum had cleared up the broken bits by the time Dad got home. So we had tea.

My Mum has this idea about eating tidily. So does my Dad.

'Manners, Joe!' she was always saying. 'You'll only choke to death if you gobble like that.'

I knew, now, it couldn't be true

because Grandma was gobbling and she handn't choked to death yet.

She seemed to me to be quite a slurpy eater, even better than Slane's dog, Messer. I expect she knew old people need building up. It was amazing how she tucked into that beefburger, specially as she didn't seem to have any teeth.

And when I saw her scrape her sprouts to the side of her plate and leave them there, just like my Mum says I'm not to, I knew I was really glad she'd come to live with us. So I scraped mine to the side of my plate and left them too.

'Eat up your sprouts, Joe!' my Mum said. 'They're good for you!'

'Brussels sprouts! Good for you?' Grandma snorted. 'I never touch them, not if I can help it. They smell bad and give you wind.'

'Grandma, dear,' my Dad began as though he was about to say something else, but then he just kept quiet.

'It's a little of what you fancy does you good, that's what,' Grandma went on. 'Better than sprouts any day.'

Grandma burped all the time, too. As well as the burping and the never eating sprouts, there were quite a few other good things Grandma did which I would have liked to do if only Mum wasn't always telling me not to. She left her things lying around on the floor so they were easier to find instead of putting them away. And she left the telly on even when she wasn't watching it. And she let the cat up on her lap to lick the plate. And she stayed in bed all morning. And she had six spoonfuls of sugar in her tea. All that sugar couldn't rot *her* teeth!

Grandma was also very thoughtful and kind-hearted. Just like me.

'I'm going to help out, just as much as I can,' she kept saying even when my Dad begged her not to.

'Nonsense, dear boy,' she said, helpfully dusting Mum's ornaments on the shelf above the fireplace while Mum was out at her Keep Fit class. 'I know that *some* old people can be a bit of a nuisance when they come to stay. Like that Mrs Whatsername Woodkins who used to live next door, where I was before, with your aunty. Interfering old bat she was. So I'm determined to help you both just as much as I can.'

'But Grandma,' said Dad. 'You're here to rest. After all, by your age you deserve it.'

'*My* age? I may have one foot in the grave but I can tell you my boy, I'm not

dead yet. I'm as tough as old boots.
Right now, I feel as young as
springtime. So I shall go on helping as
long as I'm able. And it looks to me as
though you could do with a nice cup
of tea.'

And humming cheerfully, she went
off to the kitchen to make it.

Quite soon there was a terrible smell, much worse than brussels sprouts, coming from the kitchen. It smelled rather like an old car trying to start.

'Burning rubber!' said Dad, jumping up and rushing to see if the house was on fire. I went too.

The smell, and the blue smoke, was coming from the kitchen. Grandma was sitting quietly waiting for the kettle to boil. She had the teabags in the teapot and the milk in the jug.

'Be ready in a minute, dear,' she said. 'It's just the water you have here. Seems to be taking its time to come to the boil.'

The bottom of the electric kettle was smouldering gently. Grandma hadn't plugged it into the electric socket. She'd put it on the gas stove and lit the gas underneath.

Dad turned off the gas quickly, flapped at the smoke, and opened the windows. He explained to Grandma, very carefully and slowly like he sometimes explains things to me as though I'm only three years old, that electric kettles don't go on the gas because then the rubber bits get burnt and it might cause an accident.

'*Electric* kettle?' said Grandma with surprise. 'Well I never! They all look the same , don't they? And you always *used* to use gas.'

Dad picked up the burned-out kettle, carried it outside and put it in the bin. 'Not safe to use any more,' he said. He seemed a bit upset.

So I got a saucepan, boiled some water in it, and helped Grandma make Dad a nice cup of tea to calm him down.

5 Cookery surprise

IN THE MORNING, Slane called round for me and we set out for the school bus. Halfway there I remembered my packed lunch. Dad was waiting for me on the back step. He'd got my sandwiches in his hand.

'Ooh, cheese and chutney!' I said. 'My favourite! Thanks, Dad!'

'You'll forget your own head one day, Joe!' he said.

After Mum and Dad went off to work, Grandma was left behind on her own. I'd have got bored stuck at home all day. Grandma didn't.

Mum was always telling me I ought to be more imaginative with my spare time. Grandma was very imaginative. She found lots of different things to do to be helpful.

When I got home from school, there was a note from Mum on the back door. Slane saw it first. It was for me and it was inside a sealed envelope so that Grandma wouldn't read it.

Joe, Grandma had a funny turn today. Gone to chemist to get her pills. Please can you make her a cup of tea. DON'T LET HER MAKE IT HERSELF. Back soon Love Mum

Our house was so quiet I thought Grandma must have fallen asleep in front of the telly, like Slane's Aunty Vee, who once had a funny turn, does. We tiptoed to the kitchen.

Mum's kitchen is usually so clean you could do operations in it, that's what Slane says, anyway. It didn't look like that any more.

'Wow! It's mega! Like a wizard's den!' said Slane.

There were pots and pans and mixing bowls full of different kinds of mixtures, and coloured things bubbling in saucepans.

Grandma was cooking. She'd got Mum's cook books down from the shelf, and pulled lots of packets of stuff out of the cupboards and opened some tins. She was stirring something runny in a dish.

'Ah, Joseph dear boy, just the person
I need!' she said. 'Taste this!'

'But Grandma, I think Mum said –' I
began. Mum's note on the door said I
wasn't even to let Grandma make
herself a cup of tea.

'It's for tonight,' Grandma said. 'I'm
lending a hand with the supper. Your
dear mother, she has such a lot to do,
making meals all the time.'

The stuff she wanted me to taste was brown and yellow with some bits of green in it. I didn't like the look of it.

But Slane said, 'Ooh, good, I like melted chocolate chip ice cream,' and she gave it a try. 'Mmm, it's quite interesting, really. A bit like meat stew without the meat, and a bit like treacle.'

'It's good to experiment,' said Grandma. 'I'm always having to eat sensible food. I thought we might try toffee-apples next.'

Crickey, I thought, it's going to be bad enough when Mum sees *this* mess.

'No, Grandma,' I said firmly. 'I don't think toffee-apples are a good idea. Not just now.'

But Slane said, 'Why not? They're easy –'

'No, Slane!' I said. 'And if you don't want big trouble, you better get off home quick before my Mum's back.'

6 Prize time

'IT'S ALL RIGHT, Grandma,' said Mum, after she'd got rid of the spills and cleared up the kitchen. 'I can manage with the meals from now on. So you won't need to bother tomorrow.'

She seemed a bit tense, not so much with Grandma who was only a little old lady, but more with me and then with my Dad when he got in. Although it was good having Grandma with us, I sometimes felt sorry for my Mum because these days there were always so many extra things for her to do.

'What the poor girl doesn't understand,' Grandma told me, 'is that she needs *organising* properly, then she wouldn't get so tired.' Grandma had just started to tidy up the shelves in the hall cupboard.

'Well–,' I began doubtfully, because I knew that my Mum would prefer to tidy the cupboards herself.

Grandma must have understood what I meant because, the very next day after that, she decided to think up something special to help Dad instead.

'I've found the tools,' she told me and Slane. 'Out in the shed. So I shall do a little spot of gardening for your father.' And she shuffled off across the lawn in her bedroom slippers.

And that's another thing Mum doesn't like me doing – wearing my slippers in the garden, because she says it wears them out and gets them dirty.

'Oh no, Grandma!' I said going after her. 'Dad's flowers are rather delicate. We wouldn't want to hurt them.'

'Delicate?' said Grandma. 'Nonsense!' She was already halfway to the shed.

We had to stop her. I looked at Slane. She said, 'Why don't we let her do the toffee apples instead?'

'There's no apples,' I said.

'We'll go and buy some.'

Grandma heard us and came tottering back. 'Ooh, shopping!' she said, clapping her hands together. 'I do like to get out and about!'

I said, 'No. It's too far for you to walk.'

'Nonsense,' said Grandma. 'What d'you think I am? Some lame old duck?'

She was right. After all, there wasn't much that could go wrong with a short walk along the street.

Some mornings, when I'm late, it only takes a couple of minutes to get down to the corner where me and Slane catch the school bus. But with Grandma shuffling along it seemed to take forever. I thought how my Mum was right about not wearing slippers outdoors.

Grandma loved it in the supermarket. She wanted to go down every aisle to look at everything. She wanted to buy everything, too.

'We haven't got any money for all that, Grandma,' I said, hurriedly shoving things back.

After we'd paid for the three apples, the person at the pay-counter stared at us oddly. Then she said, 'Excuse me, I just have to call the manager.'

I was really worried. 'But we haven't done anything!' I said.

'Just one moment, please.'

'Now then, young miss, we haven't got all day,' said Grandma.

I whispered to Slane, 'It's your fault, I knew something would go wrong. Let's get out quick.'

We hurried Grandma towards the exit, but before we had time to get her through the automatic door, a man in a grey suit rushed up and began to shake Grandma by the hand.

44

'Congratulations, madam, congratulations!' he said. 'Another lucky-number customer!'

Grandma didn't quite know what was going on but she seemed to like it all the same.

It was the supermarket's anniversary. Every thousandth customer received a token which they could swap for a prize.

When we saw what the prizes were, Slane said, 'Ooh, I do hope she chooses the chocolates.'

I hoped she'd choose the big basket of fruit with the fancy bow on top. She didn't choose either. Nor the radio alarm. She chose the bottle.

'Tawny port!' she said. 'That's just the ticket to put a bit of life back into your dear parents.'

By the time we'd been up to the manager's office to collect Grandma's prize, and she'd had her photo taken, she seemed very tired. Slane and I had to support her on each side all the way home. We helped her up the front step and into her armchair.

My Mum was back from work already. 'Really, Joe!' she snapped. 'Wherever have you been? She's absolutely exhausted.'

Mum seemed to think it was all my fault. Even when I'd offered her a glass of the port she was still annoyed. 'You might at least have looked after her!'

'Look after who?' said Grandma, sitting comfortably in her armchair, sipping some port. '*I* don't need any looking after. *I'm* as fit as a fiddle.'

Slane grinned and disappeared. Grandma didn't mention anything more about toffee-apples.

7 A clean ceiling

MUM AND DAD were beginning to be like middle-aged people. They were often grumpy in the evening and they never went out together like they used to. Mum said it wouldn't be safe. Dad said it wouldn't be right.

I usually got home from school before they were back from work, which was a good thing because it gave me time to clear up a bit. I knew that most days Grandma would have thought of something interesting to do, though I was never sure what sort of something it would be.

Then one afternoon when I came home from school, Grandma called out to me, 'Yoohoo, Joseph dear boy!' almost before I was in through the back door.

Grandma was on the kitchen floor. She had a stepladder and a bucket and quite a lot of water spread about so I had to take my trainers off.

Then I realised that Grandma was lying in a funny position, all crumpled up, and I knew that something worse than usual had been going on.

'Oh dear, Grandma. Have you had another funny turn?'

'No, duckie. Not now I've got those nice pills your Mum got me. No, I was just washing the ceiling. It was so dirty. I knew it needed doing.'

'The ceiling?' She was nowhere near the ceiling.

'To help your poor mother. As a
surprise. She has *such* a lot to do. Poor
girl. I was up the ladder. Then all of a
sudden, something went.'

'Went? Went where?'

'In my leg. Something cracked. I
heard it. I think I did. When I fell down
from the ladder. Maybe I should have

waited till you were back. Oh dearie me,
I do hope your mother won't be
annoyed with me.'

It was unlike Grandma to notice what
my Mum thought. I said, 'Better wait
there,' — not that she looked as though
she could go anywhere. 'I won't be
long.'

I tried Dad's number at work but he was out on a job. Luckily, just then Slane dropped by. She had a new poster of some motorcycles to give to my Grandma to stick on her bedroom wall.

I explained to Slane about Grandma washing the ceiling.

'Always up to something, your Grandma, isn't she?'

'Yeah, but this time I think it's gone a bit wrong,' I said.

When Slane saw the way Grandma was lying on the floor, all crooked and twisty, she didn't make any jokes like she usually did. She just said, 'You're right, Joe. Only one thing for it. You'll have to call in the proper authorities.'

'How?' I said. I felt too frightened inside to think straight.

So Slane dialled the 999, but she said as it was not her grandmother, but mine, I must do the talking. So I asked for an ambulance like she told me to.

A man's voice on the telephone asked if it was an emergency.

I said, 'I'm not sure.' Grandma seemed so cheerful.

He said they would be along as quick as they could. Even so, it seemed to take a long time. But Grandma didn't complain at all. If I'd just fallen off a ladder I'd have made a lot more fuss. I remembered the time I'd fallen out of an apple tree and I'd screamed so loudly that Slane said they could even hear me down at her place.

I said to Slane, 'Shouldn't we make her comfy while we're waiting?'

Slane said, 'No, you mustn't move her, not if she's injured.'

'Or make her a cup of tea?' I said. 'She always loves a good cup of tea.'

But Slane said, 'No, it's best not to do that either.'

So we went and sat on the step ladder beside her and told riddles while we waited for the ambulance to arrive. Grandma knew some of the best riddles.

Grandma was really pleased when she saw the blue flashing light on the ambulance.

'Ooh, Joseph duckie, isn't this a lark!'
she said. 'I've always wanted to be an
emergency.'

But she was annoyed they didn't use
the bell.

I went with her in the ambulance.
Slane wasn't allowed. She was mad at
that, specially as calling the ambulance
was her idea in the first place.

I held Grandma's hand and we sang songs. At least, she sang some songs and I hummed along. The ambulance man joined in a bit.

When we reached the hospital, they lifted her very carefully onto a trolley.

'Your grandma's a right corker, isn't she?' the ambulance man said to me. 'Most old folks would've been moaning their heads off.'

8 Getting going again

Mum and Dad took time off work so they could be with Grandma. They said her hip bone was broken and she would have to stay in hospital. Some days when she came home, Mum cried a bit. I think Dad did, too. I was really worried about them. But once Grandma began to get well, Mum and Dad didn't have to be there all day. They just went to visit in the evenings.

Slane and I went every day after school. On Sundays we all went together. But sometimes the nurses

asked me and Slane to go outside
because they said we were disturbing
the other patients.

We didn't mind. We knew they
didn't mean that Slane and I were
making too much noise. They meant
my Grandma was. She was always
having sing-songs and trying to get the
other patients to join in, even the ones
who were asleep.

At last she was better from the accident. But even though her bone was mended, she still couldn't walk by herself. The nurses said they must teach her to use a walking frame.

Grandma wasn't pleased.

'I've told you before! I won't be seen *dead* on one of those things,' she said. 'That's for old folk who can't walk upright.'

The walking frame was shiny metal with white plastic handles.

'Just like riding a bicycle,' I told Grandma. 'Only without the wheels.'

I zoomed round her bed to show her.

'And without the saddle,' said Slane. 'Or the pedals.'

Grandma had to learn to use it in the end. She got quite good at it, getting up speed so she could bump into doctors coming round corners.

So Slane and I went to the bike shop and bought a bike bell. Slane helped me fix it onto the handle bar.

'So you can ring it to let people know you're coming,' I said.

Grandma liked to ring it even when she wasn't going anywhere.

At home it was quiet. Not a lot happened, apart from the cat being allowed to sleep indoors again. It was

tidy, too. Mum didn't have a lot to do. We were all looking forward to Grandma coming back and cheering us up. But when she'd learned to walk again, they said she shouldn't live at our house.

'It's because of the stairs,' said Dad.

'She could sleep in the sitting room,' I said. 'Like Slane's Aunty Vee does.'

'It's not just the stairs. They say Grandma shouldn't be left on her own all day, not now she really can't cope.'

I said, 'She doesn't mind. She never gets bored. She can always think of something to do.'

'That's just the trouble. What if something *happened* to her?'

'But Grandma *likes* things happening to her!'

Dad said, 'It might be something really bad next time. They say it's not safe leaving her on her own.'

So I said I'd stay at home to take care of her.

Dad said, 'You have to go to school.'

'I don't mind missing school. Slane can come in and tell me what they've done in class.'

But they didn't think that was a good idea. Anyway, the people at the hospital had already arranged for Grandma to move to the Sunnyfields Rest Home.

'That's cruel!' I said. 'You can't make her go there. It's all full of old people half asleep. And they'd make her eat sprouts and suet puddings and things she didn't like. You can't do it. She won't like it!'

But I was wrong. Grandma loved it. She was able to have really good arguments with the other old people. They were mostly deaf so they could all

shout at each other as much as they
wanted. And in the evenings they made
it up, and played cards, and gambled for
real money. They also had outings and
videos. Grandma didn't even mind the
pink walls in the hall.

They had good teas, too. Slane and I
went to visit most days after school if
we were hungry. Slane's dog, Messer,
liked it too because there was usually a
piece of cake left over for him.

Every Sunday, Dad and Mum fetched
Grandma home for dinner.

Then, one Monday, when I got in, I
found Mum and Dad both back early
from work. Dad was upstairs shifting
furniture about and Mum was filling in
the nail holes Grandma had made.

'Hey!' I said. 'That's my workshop.'

'Not any more, son, sorry,' said Dad.
'It's going to be your Nana Pat's room
now.'

'Nana Pat!' I said. 'Olé!'

They'd had a call from Spain. Nana Pat's lonely living out there so far from home. So she's selling up and coming back to live with us. Mum was so pleased that she even began to cry a bit.

Dad gave me a hug. 'Two grans in the same town. Bit of all right, son?'

I'm really pleased. Nana Pat'll be able to teach me flamenco dancing. Maybe teach Grandma, too.